BE AN
ANIMAL EXPERT

EMILY KINGTON

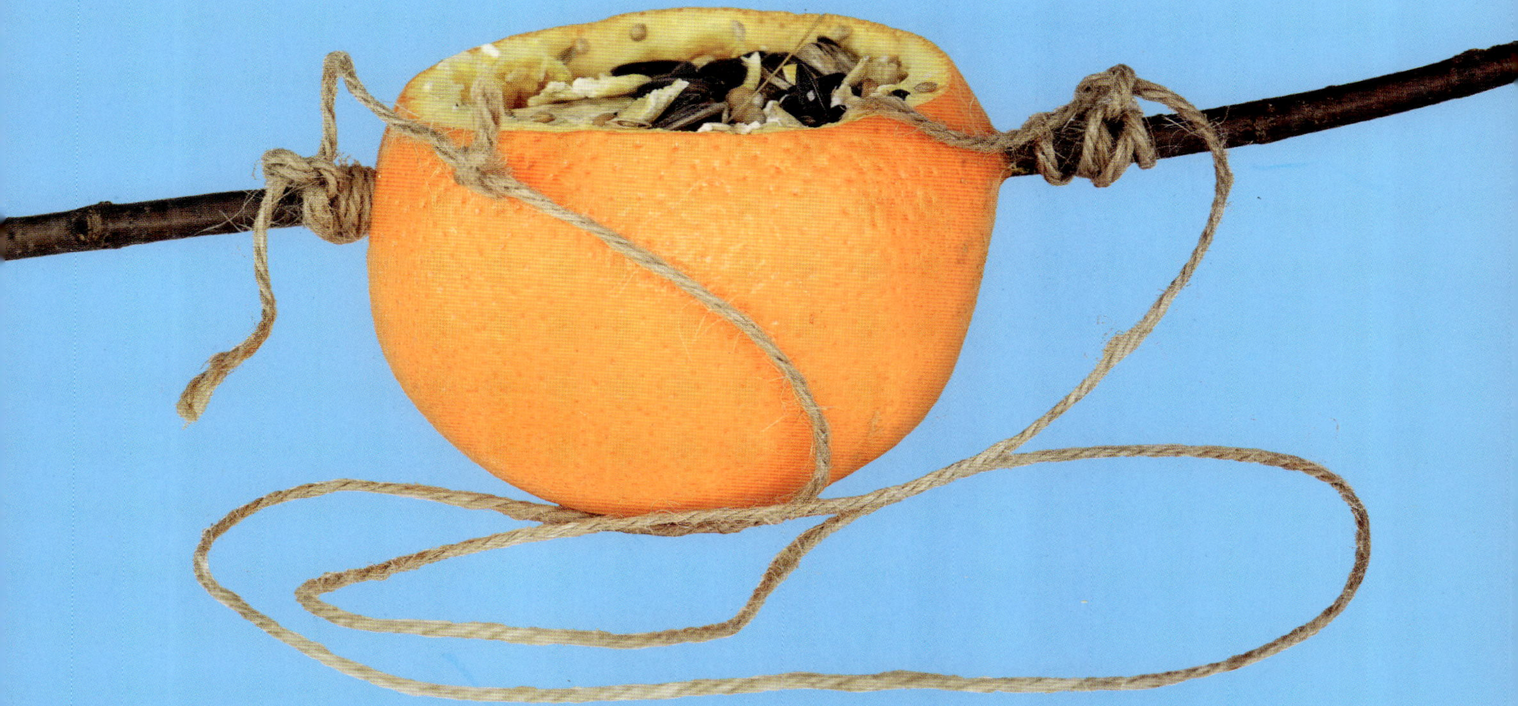

CONTENTS

Exploring the outside world and discovering what lives near you is so much better than watching television. Unplug the TV and enjoy exploring, spotting and caring for animals with a little forest fun thrown in!

Get your wellies on and take a closer look at the natural world around you. Learn how to track animals, feed and look after birds in winter, and make a woodland home for small creatures...

NATURE HUNT CHALLENGE 4

COBWEB STRUCTURE 6

HANGING NESTING BOTTLE 8

EASY BIRD FEEDER 10

WINTERY BIRD FOOD 12

CREATURE CHECKLIST 14

NEED HELP?
Watch out for this sign throughout the book. You may need help from an adult when completing these tasks.

SMALL CRITTER SHELTER 16

BE AN ANIMAL TRACKER 18

GARDEN WIND SCULPTURE 22

TAKE CARE OUT AND ABOUT 24

NATURE HUNT CHALLENGE

For some of these projects, you will need to take time out and go on a nature hunt!

NATURE HUNT SAFETY

Never go out into nature alone; make sure to always go with an adult and stay together to keep safe. It can be easy to get distracted but be careful not to get separated.

Beware, some bugs can be poisonous and may bite.

Always wash your hands after handling bugs or soil.

TAKING CARE OF THE ENVIRONMENT

Only collect nature finds from the ground. Don't pick anything off trees or plants like branches or leaves as that will damage the plant.

Treat insects with care and don't forget to release them.

GRAVEL OR SMALL STONES

Tiny stones can make great craft decorations.

SPRIGS OF LEAVES

Collect as many different shape, size and colour leaves as you can find.

STICKS

Always be on the lookout for sticks of all different sizes - they are very useful!

MOSS
Moss often grows in woods, on fallen branches or on the forest floor. Only take a little from an area where there is already a lot.

PINE CONES
Search for these on the forest floor.

VINES
Because vine stems are strong, they can be used to hold things together.

DRY GRASS OR STRAW
Collect some dry grass or straw to use for the crafts.

LOGS
Look for some small, but chunky, logs.

YOU WILL ALSO NEED:

- Gloves
- Wellington boots
- Old bag to carry items home
- Small trowel/old spoon (for collecting mud)
- Scissors (but don't use these without an adult)
- Thick paper or card
- Stiff brush
- Strong glue
- Acrylic paint
- Felt tip pens
- String
- Large, empty plastic water bottle
- Large orange
- Paper cups
- Saucepan
- Bird food (see page 10)
- Paper clay
- Rolling pin
- Cookie cutters
- Baking parchment
- Bricks
- Rake
- Wooden skewer
- Paper towel

COBWEB STRUCTURE

Make a giant cobweb around the base of a tree trunk. It makes a clever, but spooky, sculpture.

YOU WILL NEED:
- 8 long sticks
- 8 medium sticks
- 8 small sticks

1. Start by laying out the longest sticks like this around a tree trunk. The empty circle in the middle is where the tree trunk would be.

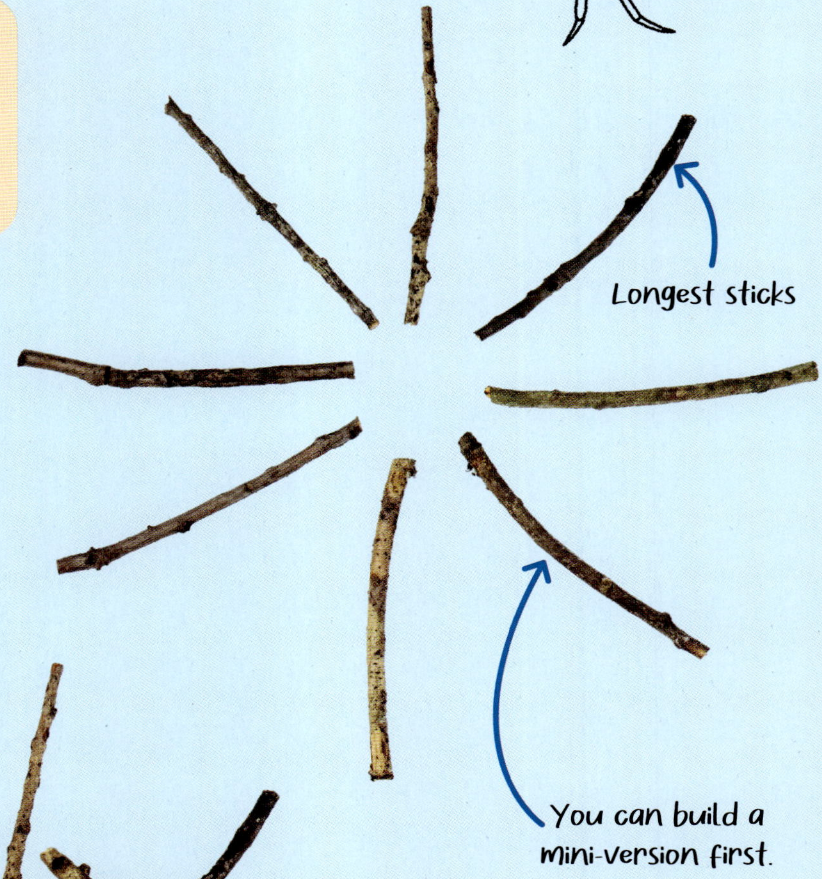

Longest sticks

You can build a mini-version first.

Smallest sticks

2. Lay the smallest sticks down in between the long sticks as shown. They don't have to be a perfect shape.

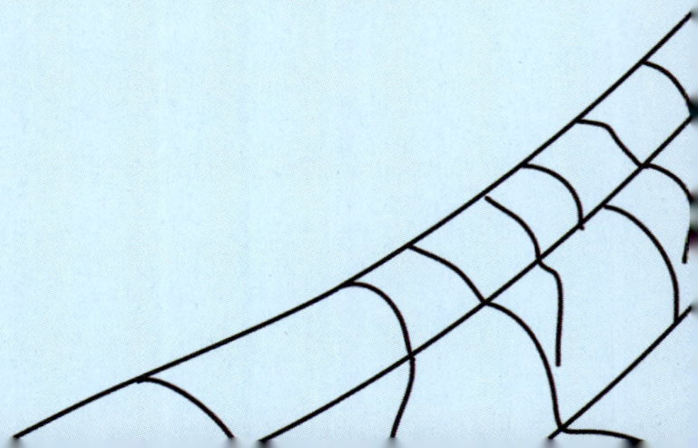

3. Lastly, lay the medium-size sticks down around the edge as shown.

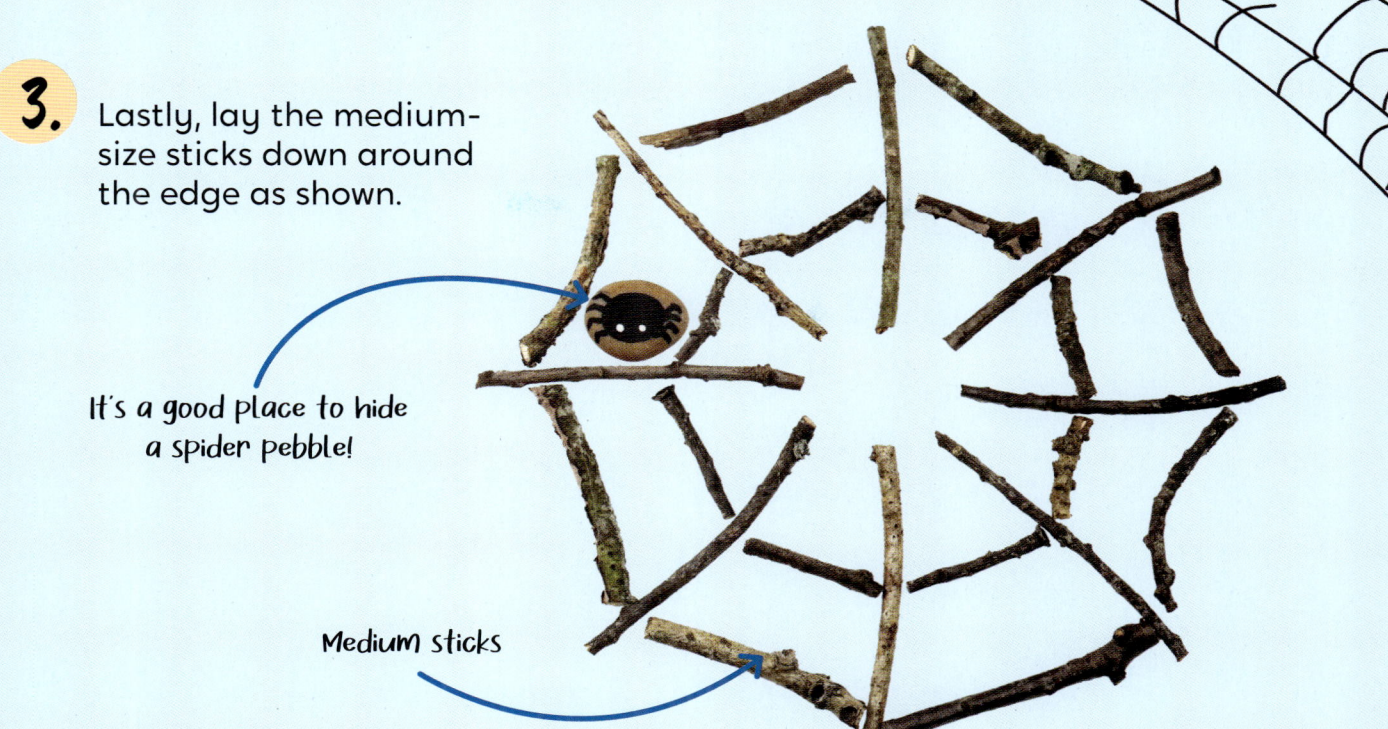

It's a good place to hide a spider pebble!

Medium sticks

NOW YOU KNOW HOW TO MAKE A COBWEB STRUCTURE, HAVE FUN BUILDING SUPER-SIZE, SPOOKY COBWEBS WHEREVER YOU GO!

DID YOU KNOW?
The silk that spiders use to build their webs is one of the strongest types of material in the world!

HANGING NESTING BOTTLE

Birds are in danger of being hunted by predators when searching on the ground for materials to build nests. Help them out by providing a hanging store of materials that they can use to build a first-class nest!

YOU WILL NEED:

- Dry grass or straw
- Moss
- Small twigs
- Large, empty water bottle
- Felt tip pen
- Scissors
- Wooden skewer
- String

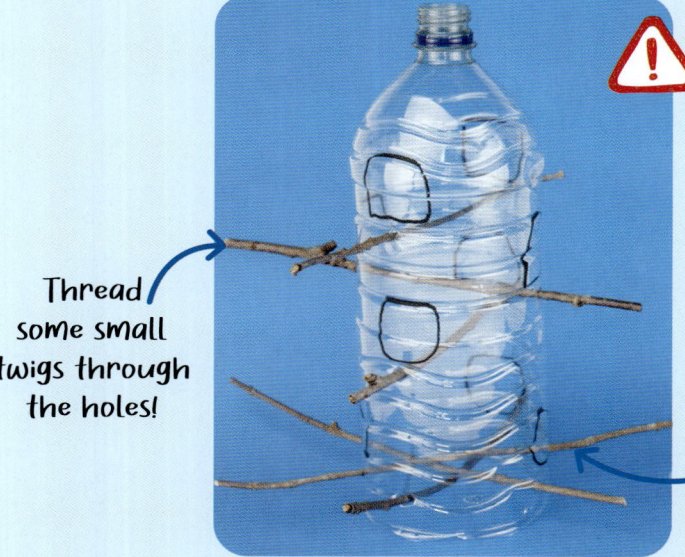

1. Ask an adult to remove the bottom of the bottle with scissors. Then ask them to make some holes all the way through the bottle with a wooden skewer. Draw some windows onto the bottle above the holes.

Thread some small twigs through the holes!

The twigs should extend outside the bottle to act as perches.

2. Ask an adult to cut out the windows with scissors. Then, fill the bottle with moss and dry grass or straw. These materials will help the birds make great, cosy nests!

Replace the bottle top to keep the contents dry.

Wrap a long piece of string around the neck of the bottle so you can hang it up.

3. Pick a good spot in your garden, and ask an adult to help you hang up your nesting bottle. Keep it topped up with moss and dry grass and straw so the birds don't run out of material for their nests!

ENJOY WATCHING YOUR NESTING BOTTLE TO SEE ALL THE DIFFERENT BIRDS THAT VISIT!

EASY BIRD FEEDER

Birds are wonderful to have in your garden. It's nice to encourage them to hang out. They also need our help in winter when food isn't as easy to find.

YOU WILL NEED:
- Small, but strong, stick
- Large orange
- String
- Food for the birds
- Wooden skewer

TOP TIP
You can buy bird seed from a pet shop, but birds also like sultanas, raisins, oats and nuts.

1. Ask an adult to cut off the top of the orange and help you scoop the insides out. Don't waste the orange insides - they make a great human snack!

This makes an excellent perch!

2. Then ask an adult to make two holes with a wooden skewer that go directly through the orange, horizontally. Push a small stick through the holes.

3. Tie a length of string onto the perch (on both sides) close to the outside of the orange. Fill the orange with a variety of bird-friendly foods and hang on the branch of a tree.

Birds will love this, and you get to eat the leftover orange!

WINTERY BIRD FOOD

Birds really do struggle to find food during a big freeze.
You can help them out by thinking ahead and making this treat for them.

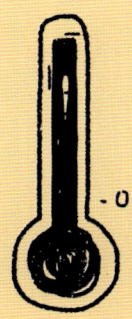

WARNING

Never put these feeders out in temperatures where the fat is likely to melt.

Melted fat that gets onto feathers will prevent a bird from being able to fly.

YOU WILL NEED:

- Paper cups
- Saucepan
- Large bowl
- Wooden skewer
- String

INGREDIENTS:

- 1 part lard to 2 parts of either: currants or sultanas; dry breadcrumbs; seeds and nuts; oats.

1. Mix together all the dry ingredients in a large bowl. Ask an adult to help you melt the lard in a saucepan. Take it off the heat and leave it to cool before mixing in the dry ingredients.

2. Ask an adult to make a small hole in the bottom of a paper cup using a wooden skewer. Thread through long string and make a big knot at the bottom.

3. Pack the mixture firmly into the cup, making sure the string stays in the middle of the mixture. Put in the fridge overnight to harden.

4. Once the mixture is hard, ask an adult to cut open the cup to reveal the solid food! They must be careful to not cut the string.

5. Store in the freezer, ready to hang on a tree branch in wintery weather.

CREATURE CHECKLIST

Here is a list of animals to spot in the wild, if you can. Some are very tricky to find, so don't expect to see them all at once!

SPOTTER'S GUIDE

Easy
These are more likely to be spotted.

Harder
These animals can be spotted if you look hard enough!

Difficult
These are really hard to spot!

ANIMAL SAFETY

Do not approach wild animals or insects. They can be dangerous!

Do not disturb animals while observing them in their habitats

Deer live in herds. If you see one, you are likely to spot others nearby!

🐾 DEER 🐾

Deer often live in forests and woods. They are most active around sunrise and dusk, but they spend the entire day foraging for food!

Birds come in all shapes and sizes.

BIRDS

How many different birds can you spot outside? You should see lots if you have made the bird feeders. If you go to a park or pond, you may see even more!

Rabbits are more active at dusk and dawn, but you can spot them during the day, too!

Foxes can even be found in towns and cities. They can be quite naughty!

RABBIT

Rabbits can be found in most parts of the world. They are social animals and live in groups in underground burrows called warrens.

FOX

Foxes live around the world in many different habitats, including forests, grasslands, deserts and mountains.

Spot frogs along the banks of streams, lakes and ponds.

These are very difficult to spot, so if you do it's a real treat!

FROG

Frogs are amphibians, which live part of their lives in water and part on land.

OTTER

Otters are the most secretive of animals, who are most active at night and will fish until dawn.

If you hear a rustle in the trees, look up. It might be a squirrel!

You will have to be as quiet as a mouse to spot these creatures.

SQUIRREL

It's scary being a squirrel – falling from the nest is a serious danger! Did you know that when they are extremely hungry, squirrels have been known to eat small birds and snakes?

FIELD MICE

These little creatures typically make burrows underground. These shelters help keep them safe from predators. But they sometimes come into our homes for food and shelter!

SMALL CRITTER SHELTER

These small woodpiles make a natural shelter and all you need to do is stack sticks and other easy-to-find materials! This quick and easy project makes a great home for wildlife of many kinds.

YOU WILL NEED:

- Large piece of wood
- Small logs
- Small branches
- Dry grass or straw
- Sticks and dry leaves
- Two bricks
- Rake

1. Firstly, decide where to build your shelter. Find a quiet, sheltered place under an evergreen bush or tree.

2. Use a rake to clear the ground and arrange the bricks and small logs as shown.

3. Lay down some dry grass or straw and leaves for bedding.

4. Balance a piece of wood across the top of the bricks to make the area underneath dark and sheltered.

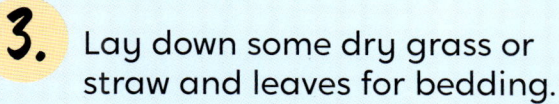

5. Camouflage the shelter by placing sticks, branches and dry leaves on the top and around the sides. Leave extra home-making materials close by for animals to use. Dry leaves and straw can be useful for making a warm bed or nest.

BE AN ANIMAL TRACKER

We may not always see the animals on our travels, but what they leave behind tells us they were there. Here are some things to look out for.

SAFETY WHEN TRACKING
Don't touch, but look out for droppings on the ground. They will tell you which animals are living nearby.

COW PATS
Cows produce funny poop that's shaped like round, flat disks. How strange!

DEER PELLETS
These round pellets are big, shiny and very dark in colour. They're usually found in clusters.

RABBIT DROPPINGS
Similar to deer pellets, rabbit droppings are round but they're much smaller!

BEAR SCAT
This poop is huge! It's usually dark, messy and filled with undigested food, like berries, seeds and animal bones.

HORSE POOP
Big animals means lots of poop! Horses leave behind big, roundish clumps of brown waste.

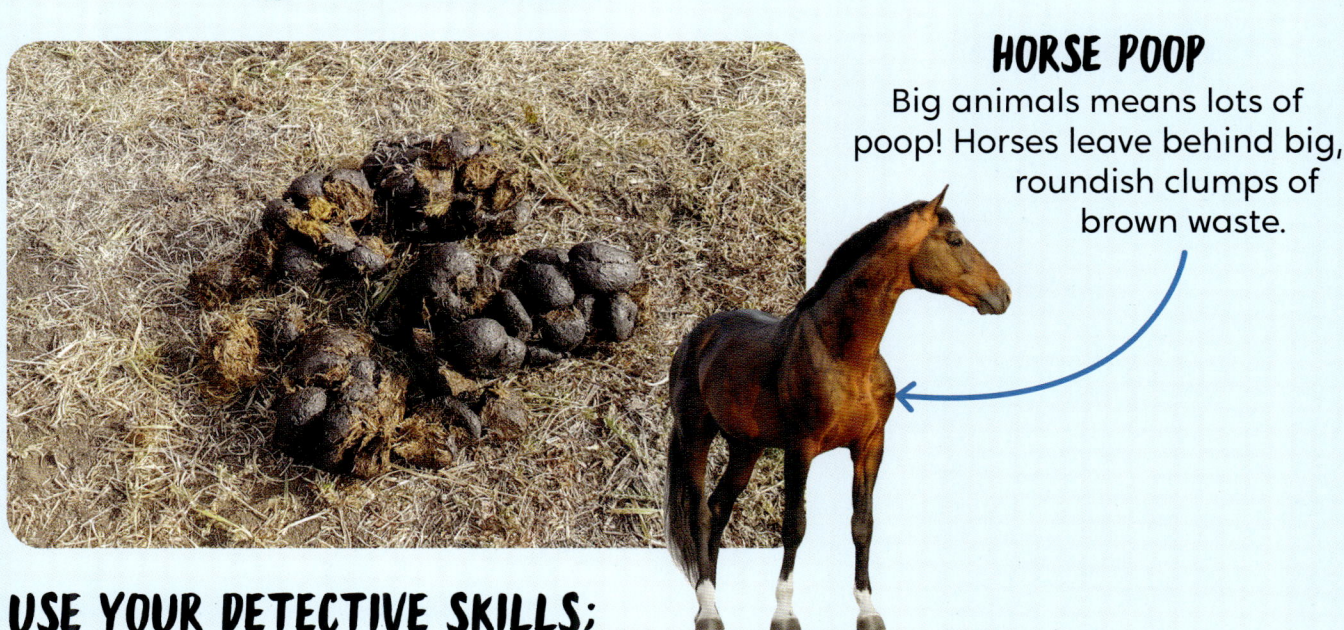

USE YOUR DETECTIVE SKILLS; IT SEEMS THAT EVERY ANIMAL'S POOP IS DIFFERENT!

ANIMAL TRACKS

When the ground is soft, look for the tracks that different animals have left behind.

DEER FOOTPRINTS

BEAR FOOTPRINTS

DOG FOOTPRINTS

BIRD FOOTPRINTS

HUMAN FOOTPRINTS

TRACKS AND FOOTPRINTS AREN'T THE ONLY SIGNS ANIMALS ARE NEARBY. THEY LEAVE BEHIND LOTS OF OTHER CLUES TOO!

MOLEHILLS
Moles burrow and raise molehills as they go, leaving little doubt that they are living nearby, underground. There never seems to be just one molehill, so you can't miss them!

SQUIRREL'S LARDER
Keep a lookout for the secret stash of a squirrel! They bury acorns and nuts underground in shallow holes, and then dig them up in winter when food is scarce.

BURROWS
Some animals, like rabbits, find safety and shelter by living underground. However, a 110-million-year-old dinosaur burrow has been discovered in Australia, so burrows are not new!

BIRD NESTS
A bird nest is the place where a bird lays and looks after its eggs and raises its young. Do not disturb birds that are nesting, but keep a lookout for them in trees and hedges.

GARDEN WIND SCULPTURE

Take a break from bird spotting or checking out nature; make a wind sculpture using all the leftover finds.

YOU WILL NEED:

- 2 strong sticks
- Cones
- Leaves
- Twigs
- Sprigs of leaves
- Small stones
- Rolling pin
- Paper clay
- Cookie cutters
- Baking parchment
- Wooden skewer or cocktail stick
- String
- Scissors

Tie four long pieces of string on each end so you can hang the finished sculpture.

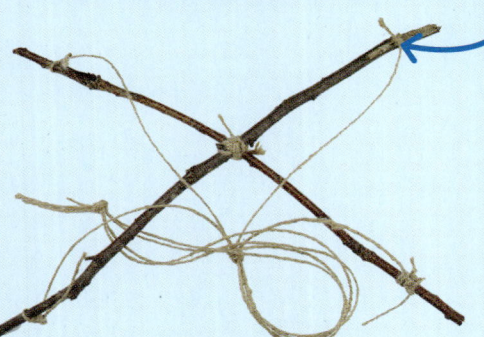

1. Make a frame by crossing two sticks, and securing them together by tying string around the middle.

2. To make your clay sculptures, roll out paper clay on a flat surface. Use cookie cutters to cut out different shapes.

Wooden skewers or cocktail sticks are the best for making holes.

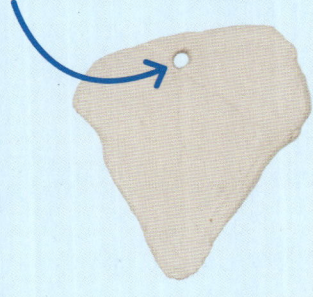

3. Ask an adult to make a small hole in each sculpture. These holes will have string threaded through eventually.

4. Decorate with some stones if you wish. Then leave your clay sculptures to dry.

5. Make natural decorations using nature finds! First, cut string to different lengths, then wind it around cones and other items.

6. Attach sprigs of leaves to sticks by winding string around them and tying knots.

Gather the four long pieces of string and knot them together.

Now you just need to hang it up in a gentle breeze.

7. Attach your decorations with different lengths of string to the main frame. Make sure they're tied on with a tight knot!

23

TAKE CARE OUT AND ABOUT

It's always brilliant fun when you are out exploring and gathering, but it's a good idea to take some things with you to stay safe.

WATER
Take plenty of water. It's easy to become dehydrated in active play.

FIRST AID KIT
Take along a basic first aid kit to deal with scratches and insect bites.

CLOTHING
Wear appropriate clothing and footwear. It can be slippery and wet in woody areas.

SAFETY FIRST

- Never eat any part of a plant or fungus or drink water from a stream.
- Climbing is fun and a real achievement, but check with adults before climbing anything and make sure they stay around to help you. It's not safe to climb alone.
- Beware of dangerous or poisonous wild plants and animals (applicable in some areas).
- Be careful near water. It can often be deeper than it looks.

ALWAYS ASK AN ADULT BEFORE YOU DO ANY OF THE PROJECTS IN THIS BOOK!

Copyright © 2024 Hungry Tomato Ltd

First published in 2024 by Hungry Tomato Ltd
F15, Old Bakery Studios, Blewetts Wharf, Malpas Road, Truro, Cornwall, TR1 1QH, UK.

No part of this publication may be reproduced, stored in a retrieval system, or transmitted in any form or by any means, electronic, mechanical, photocopying, recording, or otherwise, without prior written permission of the copyright owner.

A CIP catalogue record for this book is available from the British Library.

ISBN 9781835693575

Printed in China

Discover more at
www.hungrytomato.com

Picture credits:
Abbreviations: m-middle, t-top, l-left, r-right, bg-background.

Shutterstock: A_Lesik 19bl; Ademortuus 15tl, 17tm; Ademortuus 15tr; Aleksey Matrenin 24tm; BigPixel Photo 2tl; binik 17bl; Chris Brannon 18tl; Dmitry Pichugin 18tr; Ducu59us 17ml; Eric Isselee 14bmr, 15br, 15mr, 15bl, 15ml; fotohunter 19br; FotoRequest 14bml; Hchjjl 10tr, 12tl, 14bl, 14tl, 16t, (warning sign used throughout); KanphotoSS 17tl; Kozlik 18b; Kwadrat 17bm; Mariusgabi 2br; MR.PRAWET THADTHIAM 16tl; Parilov 4bl; photomaster 14tr, 16bm; Pkproject 24tl; prattaph 16br; Robert Hoetink 18mr; SeventyFour 3bm; Stadnret 24tr; Svietlieisha Olena 16tr; tchara 19tl; Vector Tradition (spotters guide animal footprints); Viktor Loki 17mr; WIRACHAIPHOTO 18ml; Zhukov Oleg 15tl.

Every effort has been made to trace the copyright holders, and we apologise in advance for any unintentional omissions. We would be pleased to insert the appropriate acknowledgements in any subsequent edition of this publication.